vipo®
Visits the
Swiss Alps
Why should you value others?
Ido Angel
vipo
ANIMATED STORYTIME
AV2 BY WEIGL™
ADDED VALUE • AUDIO VISUAL
POP CORN
www.av2books.com

Go to **www.av2books.com**, and enter this book's unique code.

BOOK CODE

M643282

AV² by Weigl brings you media enhanced books that support active learning.

First Published by vipo VipoLand Incorporated
32nd East Street No 3-32,
City of Panama,
Republic of Panama

Published by AV² by Weigl
350 5th Avenue, 59th Floor New York, NY 10118
Website: www.av2books.com

Library of Congress Control Number: 2015947858

ISBN: 978-1-4896-3925-7 (hardcover)
ISBN: 978-1-4896-3926-4 (single user eBook)
ISBN: 978-1-4896-3927-1 (multi-user eBook)

Editor: Katie Gillespie
Project Coordinator: Alexis Roumanis
Art Director: Terry Paulhus

Printed in the United States of America in Brainerd, Minnesota
1 2 3 4 5 6 7 8 9 0 19 18 17 16 15

082015
100715

MORAL OF THE STORY

For thousands of years, parents and teachers have used memorable stories called fables to teach simple moral lessons to children.

In the Vipo by AV² series, three friends travel to different countries around the world. They help people learn many important life lessons.

In *Vipo Visits the Swiss Alps*, Vipo and his friends teach a group of worms that they have value. The worms learn that everyone has something special to offer.

This AV² media enhanced book comes alive with...

Animated Video
Watch a custom animated movie.

Try This!
Complete activities and hands-on experiments.

Key Words
Study vocabulary, and complete a matching word activity.

Quiz
Test your knowledge.

AV² Storytime Navigation

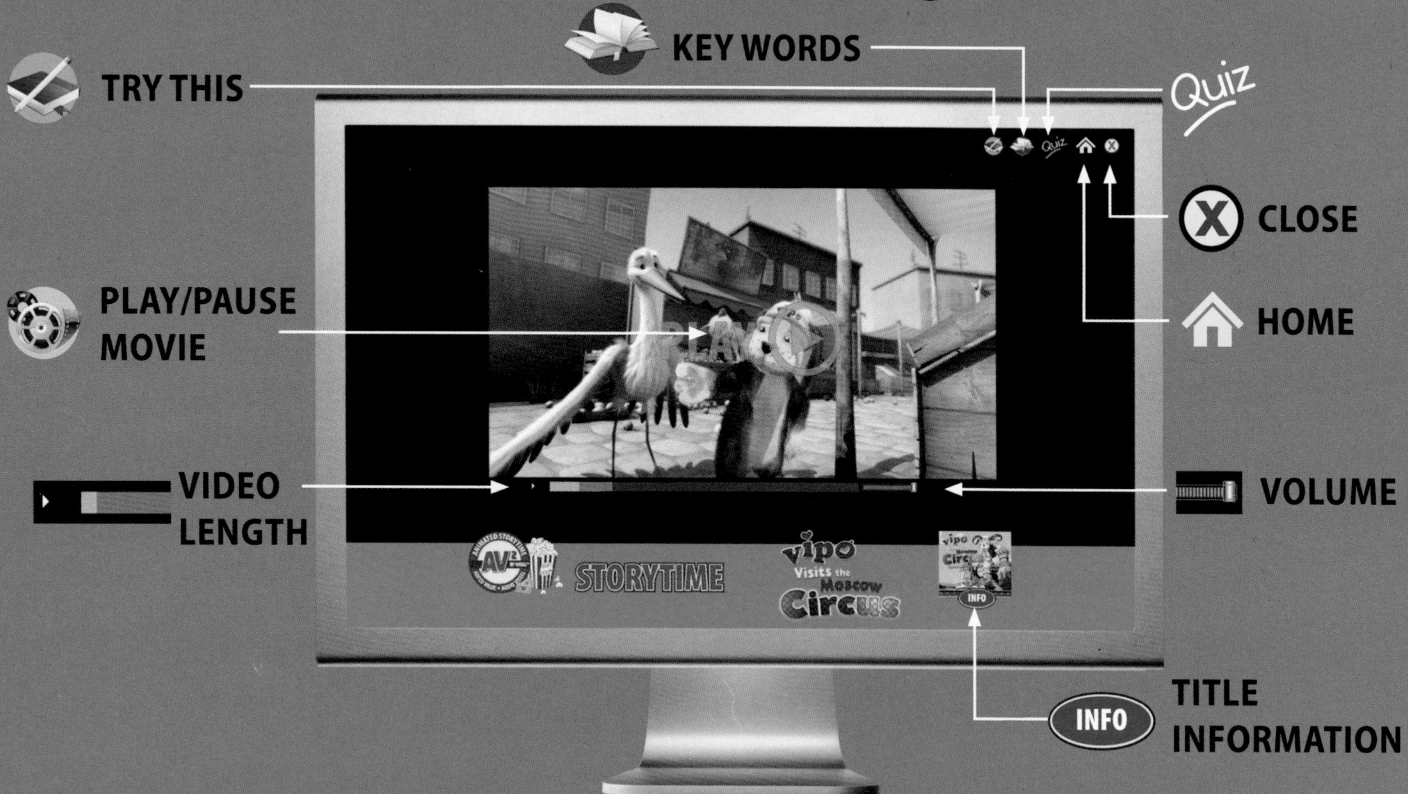

The Characters

Henry
I am a stork. I like going on adventures with Vipo. I am curious about the world.
Betty
I am a cat. I like to make friends with people from many different places. I like to help others.

The Story

Vipo, Henry, and Betty were flying over the Swiss Alps.
"I've always wanted to visit Switzerland," said Henry.
"Let's have some fun in the snow," said Vipo.
"Look," said Henry. "There are sleds outside of that cabin."
"Let's go and ask if we can borrow them," said Vipo.

vipo

They opened the door and saw a man spraying the walls.
"Hi!" said Vipo. "Can we borrow those sleds outside?"
"Sure," said the man. "And take these useless worms with you! No one wants them around."
"No thanks," said one of the worms. "We want to stay here and eat."
"I wish you'd stop eating my cabin," said the man.

The three friends jumped on the sleds and raced down the mountain.
"You'll never catch me!" teased Betty.
Betty turned to look at Vipo and Henry behind her.
"Watch out!" yelled Vipo.
Betty flew over a large cliff.
"Help!" cried Betty.
Vipo and Henry raced after her.

Betty landed in the snow and started to roll.
As she rolled, snow stuck to her body.
"I can't stop!" cried Betty.
"Don't worry," said Henry. "We'll help you."

Vipo and Henry tried to stop Betty.
"Oh no!" said Vipo. "I'm stuck."
"Me too!" called Henry.
The three friends turned into one big snowball.

The snowball rolled faster and faster down the mountain.
"How can we stop?" asked Henry.
"Try flapping your wings," Betty suggested.
"It's not working," replied Henry.
"We're heading straight for that building," cried Vipo.
"Watch out!" Betty cried as they crashed into the building.
The snowball broke apart, freeing the three friends.

Inside the chocolate factory, the crash bumped the hands of the clock from one o'clock to four o'clock. The chocolate maker woke with a start.

"Oh my!" he said. "I slept in. It is time to put more chocolate in the machine."

The chocolate maker put a full load of chocolate into the machine.
"That doesn't look right," he said.
The machine started to make a buzzing sound.
"I put too much chocolate in the machine," he said.
The machine began to rattle and shake.
"Oh no!" he yelled. "It's going to blow!"
The chocolate maker ran outside as fast as he could.

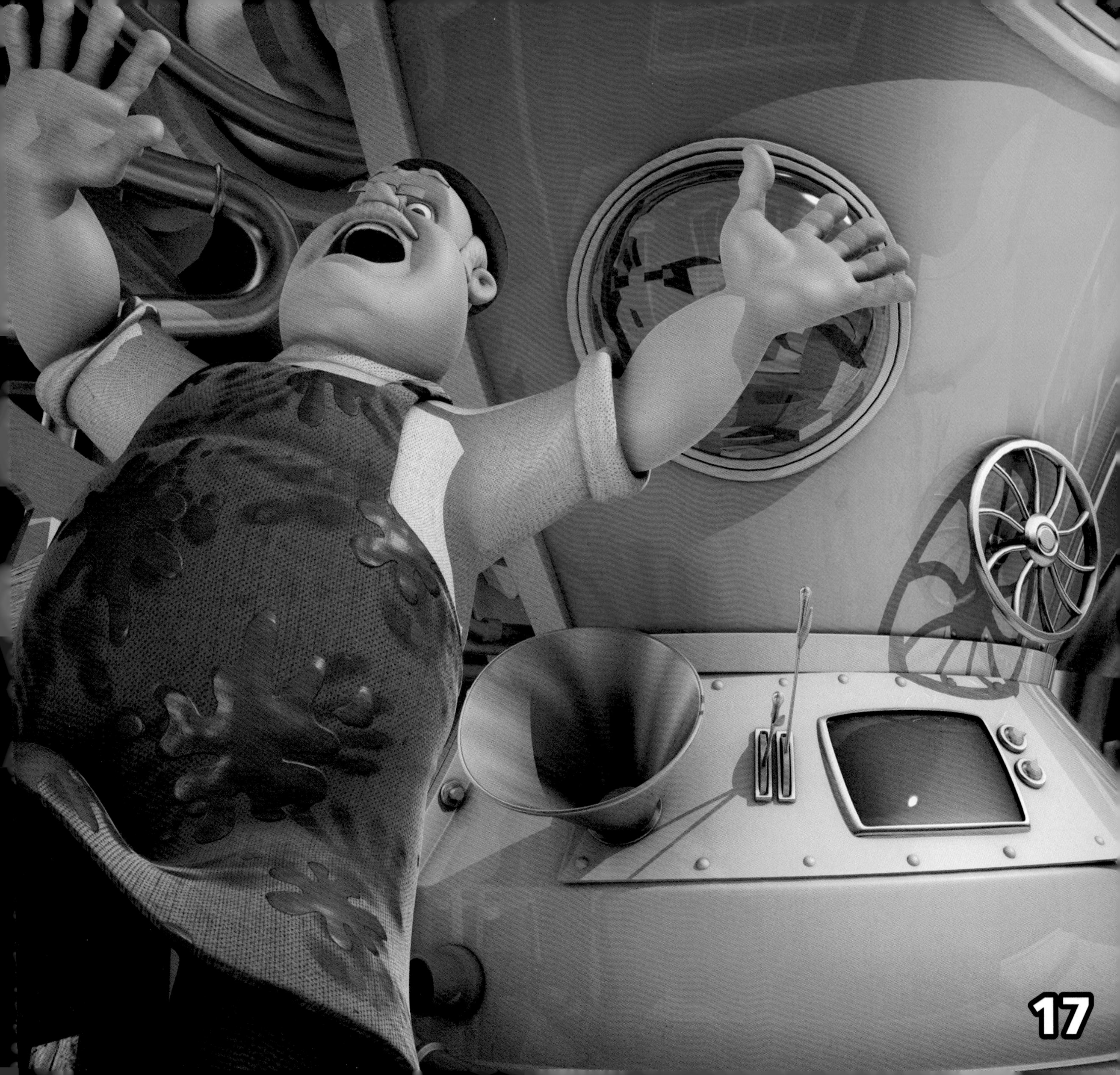

Chocolate came shooting out of the factory and flowed down the mountain.
The chocolate cooled quickly in the snowy weather.
Many skiers got stuck in the hardened chocolate.
"Oh no!" said Henry. "What can we do to help them?"
"We could eat the chocolate," Betty suggested.
"Wait!" said Vipo. "The worms love to eat! Let's go get them."

Vipo, Henry, and Betty returned with bags full of worms.
"There it is, as promised," said Vipo.
Vipo and Henry emptied the bags onto the mountain.
"Chocolate!" cried the worms. "Thank you!"
The worms ate the chocolate, freeing the skiers.
"Wow," said Betty. "It's working, Vipo."
The grateful skiers thanked the worms for freeing them from the chocolate.

"See, that man was wrong about you," said Betty.
"People do want you around!"
"Everyone has value," said Vipo.
"They sure can eat a lot of chocolate!" Henry laughed.

Moral of the Story

It is best to value others.
Everyone has something special to offer.

Quiz

1 Why was the man spraying the cabin?

2 Who went flying off a cliff?

3 Who got stuck in a giant snowball?

4 What time was the clock changed to?

5 Why did the chocolate machine blow up?

6 Who ate all of the chocolate?

Answers:

1. He was trying to get rid of the worms
2. Betty
3. Vipo, Henry, and Betty
4. Four o'clock
5. The chocolate maker put too much chocolate in the machine
6. The worms

Check out www.av2books.com for your animated storytime media enhanced book!

1. Go to www.av2books.com
2. Enter book code **M643282**
3. Fuel your imagination online!

www.av2books.com

AV² Storytime Navigation

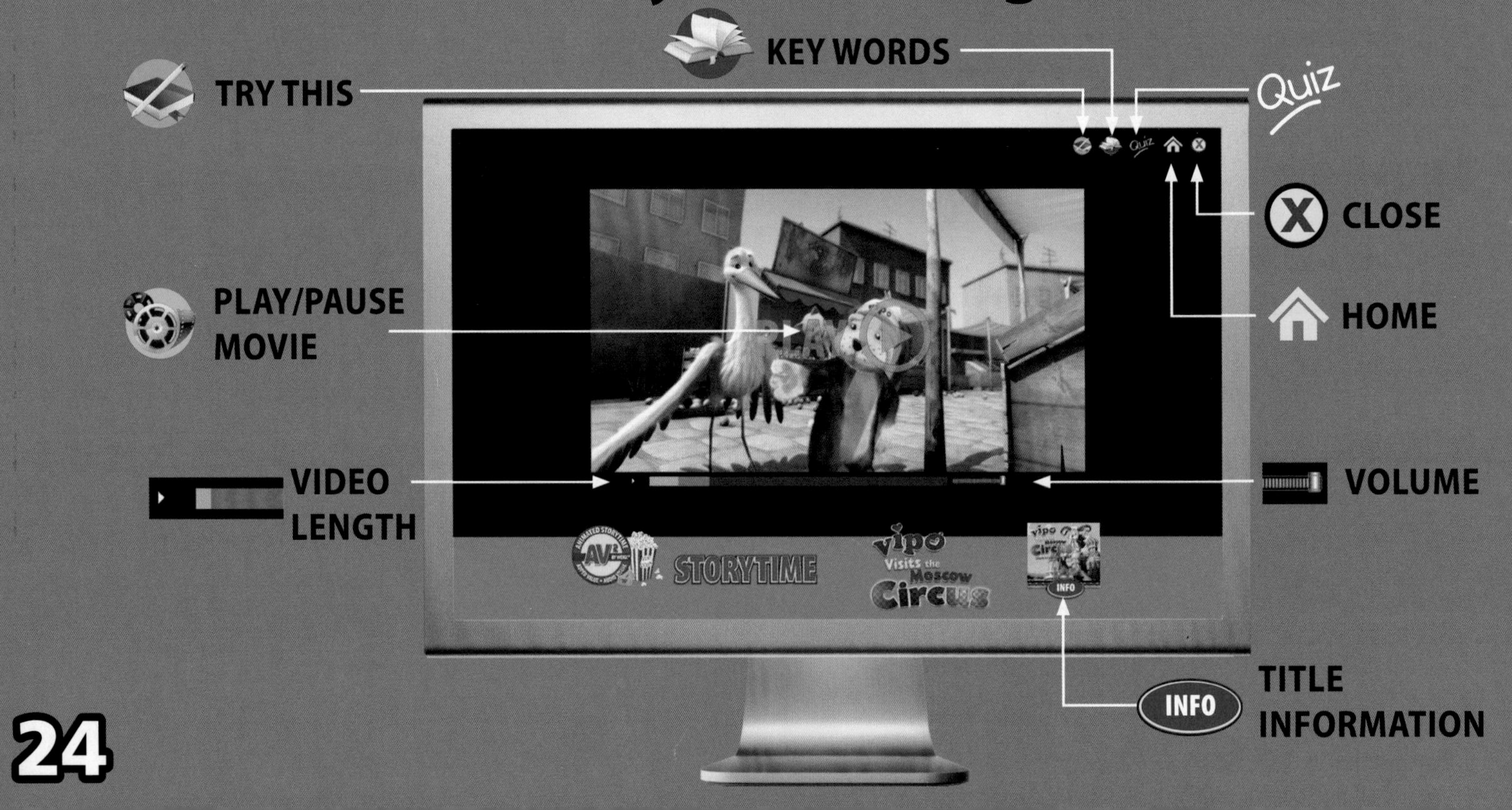